Strange Light

Leo John

First Edition April 2025.

Copyright @2025 Leo John.

All rights reserved.

This book is sold subject to the condition that it shall not, by way of trade or otherwise, be lent, resold, hired out or otherwise circulated in any form of binding or cover other than in which it is published and without similar conditions including this condition being imposed upon the subsequent purchaser. Copyright @2025

Leo John.

For all of you out there who enjoy a little escapism, laced with a macabre sense of fun. Leo John.

Chapter 1: Mundane Monday.

The air was heavy, with the scent of damp earth and decaying leaves. Sunlight, fractured and weak, filtered through the dense canopy above, casting long, skeletal shadows across the forest floor. It was a place of profound silence, broken only by the occasional rustle of unseen creatures and the distant, almost imperceptible creak of ancient trees shifting in the breeze. For the solitary wanderer, this was sanctuary, a refuge from the relentless pressure of human society. I found solace in the solitude, a peace that settled deep within my bones, a balm against the anxieties that gnawed at the edges of my mind.

I walked a well-worn path, my boots sinking slightly into the soft earth. The path, barely more than a suggestion in the undergrowth, wound its way deeper into the heart of the woods, leading me away from the edges of civilization, further into the embrace of the primeval wilderness. I carried no map, no compass, no phone. I didn't need them. I knew this wood, or at least a part of it, intimately. It was a familiar labyrinth, a comforting maze of twisted branches and mossy stones.

However, today a different feeling shadowed the familiar comfort. A subtle dissonance hummed beneath the surface of the tranquillity, a prickling unease that spread through me like a cold shiver. The silence, once soothing, now felt oppressive, heavy with an unspoken menace. The shadows seemed to lengthen, to writhe and twist, taking on a life of their own. The usual comforting sounds of the forest – the chirping of crickets, the rustling of leaves – were muted, replaced by an unsettling stillness, punctuated by the occasional, unsettling snap of a twig, far too loud, far too distinct in the otherwise silent wood. Structures pulsating with internal light, were no longer just unsettling: they were breathtaking. They were a testament to a level of technological sophistication far beyond our comprehension, a level where technology and nature were not opposed but intertwined, a harmonious blend of the organic and the inorganic. Let's rewind to a couple of hours prior on this mundane Monday…

"We're letting you go!"

Despair enveloped me as the realization I was unemployed hit me. The conversation was short and to the point – I was to clear my desk, and leave, redundancy smirking at me as the weight of liquidation fell on my shoulders; fell on everyone's shoulders; destroying us all quietly in a moment. The mortgage on my modest home refusing to vanish from my thoughts; the forthcoming direct debits refusing to vanish from my thoughts; the desperation refusing to vanish from my thoughts! Redundant! No future paychecks or lump sum, given our company had been forcibly closed. A shocking horror encompassed my soul, and I found myself driving; driving; driving some distance to the woodlands. A slice of time to clear my head, a wave of fresh air, a moment to think things through in an urban paradise.

Silence. Solitude. Serenity. Walking mindlessly, aimlessly through the verdant emerald foliage. Birds twittering, singing without a care in the world. Oh, to be a winged creature right now – the freedom to fly high, without the constraints of humanity's civilisation constricting every moment of life! A lone raven perched in a tree, liquid eyes focused in my direction, an inquisitive stance.

"Hey!" I call, unsure as to why, as I was certainly not expecting a reply. It stared at me, raping my soul with its direct deep reading of my psyche. I chuckled a little. The raven: an ebony, tar feathered raven. Beautiful, mysterious, wild. My heart, usually a steady drum against my ribs, began to quicken. I tried to rationalize the growing fear, telling myself it was just the fading light, the encroaching darkness, the natural anxieties of being alone in such a remote place. Yet, a deeper unease lingered, a sense of being watched, a prickling feeling on the back of my neck that spoke of something unseen, something malevolent lurking just beyond the periphery of his vision.

I pressed on, the path seeming to twist and turn in unpredictable ways, as if deliberately trying to disorient me. The trees, once familiar companions, now loomed over me like menacing sentinels, their gnarled branches clawing at the twilight sky. My depression swamped me. The air grew colder, a damp chill that seeped into my bones, chilling me to the marrow. The scent of decaying leaves intensified, morphing into something more pungent, something vaguely metallic and nauseating.

I paused, my breath misting in the cool air. I listened, straining to hear any sound above the frantic beat of my heart. The silence was unnerving, broken only by the distant, mournful call of an unseen bird – a sound both haunting and strangely unsettling. It was a sound I didn't recognize, a melody of despair woven into the fabric of the forest's stillness.

I felt a surge of primal fear, a deep-seated instinct screaming at me to turn back, to flee the encroaching darkness. However, almost perverse curiosity held me captive, a morbid fascination that compelled me to continue deeper into the heart of the wood. I knew, on some level, that something was waiting for me, something terrible and inescapable. The path beckoned, a dark ribbon unwinding into the heart of the unknown.

As I walked, a sense of disorientation began to creep in. The trees seemed to shift and sway, their forms blurring at the edges of his vision. The familiar path twisted and turned, becoming less a guide and more a cruel labyrinth, designed to trap him. The air grew heavy with a strange, almost electrical tension, a palpable hum that vibrated in his bones. I felt a growing sense of dread, a certainty that I was being watched, that something was tracking my every move.

The twilight deepened, swallowing the last vestiges of light. The forest became a dark and suffocating maze of intrigue, a place where shadows danced and whispered secrets in the rustling leaves. I stumbled, my foot catching on a hidden root, sending me sprawling to the forest floor. As I scrambled to my feet, a blinding light erupted from the sky, an intense, white brilliance that seared my eyes and filled me with a sense of utter helplessness.

I suddenly became aware of a low humming sound. I looked around but saw nothing. Then there were many lights, shining brilliantly in my direction, illuminating the forest which was now bathed in twilight. Suddenly a metallic, symmetrical object appeared above me, radiating light. I screamed a silent, wordless cry which was lost in the maelstrom of blinding light! Rays of light caught me, and I felt myself levitating off the ground towards this strange craft. Crimson lights encircled sapphire beams; the whole surreal situation bizarre. Was this it – was I finally having a nervous breakdown? But no – every chamber in my head screamed “Leave! Run!” but I couldn’t. I was floating through the air, and with horror realised I was being carried by beings which were non-human and not of this earth! I was being abducted by aliens!

The light enveloped me, a searing wave of energy washed over me, stripping away my sense of self, my sense of place. I felt a wrenching sensation, a tearing apart of my very being, as if I were being pulled apart at the molecular level. I screamed, a silent, wordless cry lost in the maelstrom of blinding light and unbearable pressure. My body convulsed, my muscles contracting and relaxing in a wild, spasmodic rhythm.

Then, as suddenly as it had begun, the light vanished, leaving me shrouded in a suffocating darkness. I lay there, broken, disoriented, my senses reeling from the assault. I couldn't tell where I was, what had happened, or even who I was. I was adrift in a sea of confusion and fear, utterly lost and utterly alone. The silence, once a source of peace, now felt like a tomb, pressing down upon me, crushing me beneath its weight. I was alone, trapped, utterly at the mercy of something unseen, something unknowable, something utterly terrifying. The wood, once a sanctuary, had become a prison. The abduction was complete. The nightmare had just begun!

I felt a throbbing pain in my head, a dull ache that pulsed in rhythm with my racing heart. The darkness around me was absolute, devoid of any light or sound, except for a low, almost imperceptible hum that vibrated through the floor and up into his body. The feeling was strange, deeply unsettling, as if the very ground beneath me was alive, teeming with a hidden energy. The air was still, heavy, and strangely metallic, carrying with it a faint, nauseating odor that triggered a wave of nausea.

The imaginary clock ticked and after what seemed like an eternity, there was a shift, a subtle change in the texture of the darkness. With a sudden lurch, the darkness gave way. I gasped as my eyes flickered open, vision slowly adjusting to the strange, light that bathed me in its eerie glow. The environment unlike anything I had ever seen or even imagined.

I found myself in a vast, cavernous space, the walls and ceiling constructed from a material that looked like polished obsidian, reflecting the light in a multitude of shimmering facets. The air was thick with an unfamiliar scent, a blend of ozone and something faintly floral, yet somehow unsettlingly alien. Before me lay a sprawling landscape of bizarre and terrifying creatures, confined within enclosures of strange, alien architecture.

Chapter 2: The Slow Creep of Adaptation

I was inside a craft of some sort. Metallic furnishings humming and spinning; watery figures floating to and fro, often hovering next to me, seemingly inspecting their new acquaintance. The initial terror, a visceral, primal scream trapped within my throat, slowly ebbed. It didn't vanish entirely, not at first. Instead, it morphed, transmuting into a low, persistent hum of unease that vibrated beneath the surface of my consciousness.

These beings, with their unsettling obsidian skin and silent communication, remained unnerving, but their strangeness began to lose its sharp edges. The constant, unwavering observation, initially a source of paralyzing fear, became a kind of morbid fascination. They were glued to me, and I found myself also observing them - with many of these characters, all humming and chattering in a language that I couldn't comprehend. It was mesmerizing to me to second guess their conversation. Huge eyes appeared to telepathically attempt communicating with me that there was nothing to be afraid of, to relax! Again, I questioned my sanity…was this real? And yet I was simply allowed to be.

I found myself studying them, not with the frantic desperation of a prisoner yearning for freedom, but with the detached curiosity of a scientist observing a rare specimen. I noticed patterns in their seemingly random movements, a subtle choreography underlying the chaotic ballet of light. This was the beginning of my new life…

After a while I noticed their gatherings, although terrifying, gradually revealed a peculiar logic, a complex system of signals and responses that, over time, began to resemble a structured ritual. There was a resonant hum that emanated from the ground during these apparent social occasions, and they were no longer a source of dread, but became a hypnotic pulse that synchronized with my own heartbeat, a strange form of involuntary empathy.

Time drifted and it seemed that I had been there for eternity. Their social structures, initially baffling, started to reveal a strange coherence. What I initially perceived as chaos was a highly organized system of interconnectedness. They seemed to operate as a single organism, a collective consciousness where everyone played a specific role, a cog in a vast, intricate machine. The precision of their movements, their synchronized actions, spoke of a level of societal cohesion that dwarfed anything I had witnessed in human society. Their seeming lack of leadership wasn't an indication of anarchy, but a testament to their unique form of communal governance, a complex web of interconnectedness that operated without the need for central authority. Their technology, so profoundly alien at first, also began to yield its secrets. I observed the seamless integration of their knowledge with the living planet, the symbiotic relationship between their creations and the natural environment. The buildings, those organic structures pulsating with internal light, were no longer just unsettling: they were breathtaking. I had no idea where I was or what was happening, but I had stopped being afraid. They were a testament to a level of technological sophistication far beyond our comprehension, a level where technology and nature were not opposed but intertwined, a harmonious blend of the organic and the inorganic.

As I became aware of my surroundings, I noticed strange pictures adorning walls. Art, which I initially found grotesque, but then they began to resonate with me on a deeper level. The bioluminescent paintings, with their abstract and dreamlike forms, began to evoke not just unease but also a strange sense of beauty. The sculptures, carved from living rock and pulsating fungi, were a grotesque parody of natural forms, yet held a compelling, almost hypnotic appeal. It was art that challenged my preconceptions, pushing the boundaries of my understanding of aesthetics, shattering my preconceived notions of what art should be…or should I say what life should be?

Mealtimes also became a matter of interest, the food a collection of bioluminescent fungi and pulsating plants, remained unsettling in its appearance. But the taste… that was a revelation! The flavors, complex and strange, were a symphony of sensations that defied earthly description. It was nourishment, sustenance, a connection to this extra-terrestrial world, a silent acceptance of its reality. With each meal, my sense of otherness diminished, replaced by a sense of belonging, however tenuous.

Even sleep began to transform. The city's gentle hum, the subtle shifts in light, the rhythmic pulsing of my enclosure's walls – all combined to induce a deep, restorative sleep unlike any I'd ever experienced. It was a slumber governed by the planet's rhythms, a sleep that nourished me on a cellular level. The dreams I experienced were as bizarre and wondrous as the world around me, filled with images and sensations that stretched the limits of my imagination. These dreams, far from being disturbing, were often strangely comforting, a testament to the power of the alien environment to shape my mind, to rewire my perceptions of reality.

The Things (as I called them) themselves became more than just observers. Their silent observation wasn't mere surveillance; it was a form of communication, a subtle exchange of information that bypassed conventional language. I began to understand their bioluminescent displays, their silent symphony of light, not intellectually, but on some level at least.

I became a watcher – the irony of the watched being watched whilst watching. I found myself studying them, not with the frantic desperation of a prisoner yearning for freedom, but with the detached curiosity of a scientist observing a rare specimen. I noticed patterns in their seemingly random movements, a subtle choreography underlying the chaotic ballet of light.

The social structures of The Things, at first baffling, started to reveal a strange coherence. What I had perceived as chaos, as aforesaid, was a highly organized system of interconnectedness. They seemed to operate as a single organism, a collective consciousness where everyone played a specific role, a cog in a vast, intricate machine. Every now and then I attempted a dialogue.

"Please don't hurt me!" always met with what appeared to be amusement. I was there to amuse them! They never uttered anything intelligible, but I always felt a sense of telepathy.

"Relax. We mean you know harm." And I sensed their laughter.

The Things themselves became more than just observers. Their silent observation wasn't mere surveillance; it was a form of communication, a subtle exchange of information that bypassed conventional language. I began to understand their bioluminescent displays, their silent symphony of light, not intellectually, but viscerally, an intuitive comprehension that bypassed the limitations of my rational mind. It was a language spoken through feeling, through intuition, through a connection that transcended words.

Their detachment, I realized, wasn't cold; it reflected their unique perspective, a way of observing and processing information that differed vastly from our own. They were scientists, but scientists driven by a sense of wonder and curiosity, rather than a need for control or dominance. Their fascination with categorization, their need to understand and analyse, was ultimately a testament to their capacity for empathy, a desire to understand the universe and their place within it.

My own transformation, a slow, creeping metamorphosis, was underway. It was not a sudden shift, but a gradual reshaping of my perceptions, my beliefs, my very identity. The process was subtle, almost imperceptible, but undeniable. The sharp lines of fear were blurring, replaced by the muted tones of acceptance, even fascination. The alien world was no longer merely hostile; it was becoming home. The Things, my captors, were becoming something else entirely: something akin to… guides.

The artifact, the intricately carved metallic object, remained a focal point of my curiosity. I spent hours studying its enigmatic symbols, trying to find a pattern, a clue, a connection. It was a tangible link to this alien world, a bridge between my past and my present, a symbol of my transformation. The symbols themselves remained indecipherable, but their very existence was a source of comfort, a tangible connection to a reality far removed from my own.

The slow creep of adaptation wasn't simply a physical or mental process; it was a spiritual journey, a stripping away of ingrained beliefs, a shedding of old identities, to make way for something new. My human experience, once the foundation of my existence, was gradually being replaced by something different, something profoundly strange and yet strangely comforting. This was an adaptation not just to a new environment, but to a new way of being, a new perspective on life, death, and the very nature of existence. The end of my transformation was far from sight, but I found myself strangely eager to see what lay ahead, what new forms of existence this strange and beautiful world held in store for me. I had been taken – why me? Because I was there – in the wrong place at the wrong time – I was simply there! Initially terror seized me but dissipated as I recognized I would not be harmed, just kept for observation. We are all being observed; we're just not necessarily aware of it!

Chapter 3: Gradual Downfall.

The creatures were grotesque parodies of life, a horrifying menagerie of creatures that seemed plucked from the darkest corners of his nightmares. There were creatures with skin like molten metal, others with eyes that glowed with an inner light, and still others with bodies that shifted and pulsed in a terrifying display of alien biology. I could make out snippets of other human-like figures within the cages. They exhibited the same sense of hopeless captivity, their eyes filled with a dull, resigned fear thrown in my direction, but difficult to read. But were they human? I couldn't fully tell...just vaguely see dark shapes resembling homo-sapiens in form. I assumed they were people. All I could do was shake my head, still reeling from the shock. No idea where I was, what planet, what universe? Entirely alone. The prison was not the forest anymore, but the strangest zoo imaginable. And the unsettling part is I was one of the exhibits.

The light was not a gentle illumination; it was an assault. It wasn't merely bright; it was a searing white inferno that burned into our retinas, leaving us blind, not to darkness, but to the world as we knew it. The pressure was immense, a crushing weight that squeezed the air from our lungs, making each breath a desperate, agonizing struggle. I felt myself being pulled apart, stretched and distorted, as if some invisible forces were tearing me at the atomic level. My bones ached, my muscles spasmed, and a searing pain ripped through my body, paralyzing me with agony.

There was no sound, not in the usual sense. Instead, a high-pitched whine, a resonant vibration that penetrated deep into the skull, assaulting from all directions. It wasn't an auditory experience; it was a physical one, a feeling that resonated in the very marrow of my bones, a visceral, terrifying tremor that threatened to shatter me from the inside out. Awareness fractured, splintering into a thousand pieces, each fragment a tiny shard of agonizing pain and disorientation.

Time became a thing of the past. Seconds stretched into hours, minutes became eons, and the boundaries of reality blurred and dissolved. I was losing my sense of self, my identity dissolving into the maelstrom. All thoughts, usually a clear stream of consciousness, became fragmented, erratic, and nonsensical. Fear, pure, unadulterated terror, consumed me. “Help!” fell on deaf ears. “Help.” None came.

Then, as suddenly as it began, the assault fear had commenced, stopped! The light vanished, the pressure eased, and the agonizing pain subsided. In its place was a profound sense of disorientation. I was adrift, suspended in a void, senses reeling from the sheer brutality of the experience. I didn't know where I was, what had happened, or even who I was.

I attempted to move, but my limbs felt heavy, unresponsive. I felt like a broken doll, its joints dislocated, its components scattered and disconnected. The darkness was absolute, utterly devoid of any sensory input, except for the faint, almost imperceptible tremor that still resonated within my very being. The silence was unnerving, a suffocating blanket that pressed down, crushing me beneath its weight. It was a silence that spoke of isolation, of utter loneliness, a silence that amplified the fear that gnawed at the edges of the conscious mind.

A low hum, like the drone of a distant machine, began to build, slowly intensifying until it vibrated through my body, shaking me to the very core. I felt a creeping sensation, a crawling feeling on my skin, as if thousands of tiny insects were dancing beneath the epidermis. I sensed a change in the pressure, a difference in the temperature, a shift in the very fabric of reality itself. I felt myself being moved, carried, perhaps even floating, suspended in some form of unknown conveyance. Utterly helpless, entirely at the mercy of whatever force had abducted me.

The hum intensified, reaching a fever pitch, and then, as suddenly as it had begun, it stopped. A wave of nausea swamped me, and a sharp pain in pierced my head, followed by a disorienting rush of images, colors, sounds, and sensations that overwhelmed. It was a sensory overload of unimaginable proportions, a chaotic torrent of data that assaulted the mind and shattered the already fragile sense of self.

Slowly my vision began to clear. The darkness gave way to a strange, ethereal light, a soft, pulsating glow that illuminated the vast, cavernous space in which I found himself. I felt a weightlessness, a sense of being suspended in mid-air, as my body slowly descended to the ground. The ground beneath my feet was surprisingly firm, cool, and smooth, composed of some unknown material that felt strangely organic. I looked around, and the sheer strangeness of the surroundings momentarily paralyzed me with awe. I was now in a vast chamber, the walls and ceiling constructed from a shimmering, obsidian-like material that reflected the ethereal light in a dizzying array of patterns and colors. The air was thick, heavy, and tasted metallic, carrying with it the faint scent of ozone and something else – a strange, floral aroma that held a subtle undercurrent of something unsettlingly alien. Before me stretched a vast landscape, not of trees and fields, but of strange, alien structures and enclosures. These were unlike anything I had ever seen, unlike anything I could even begin to comprehend. They were sleek, elegant, and impossibly smooth, composed of materials that seemed to defy the laws of physics. Within these enclosures were... more creatures. More grotesque, terrifying creatures that seemed plucked from the darkest corners of the imagination. Some had skin like molten metal, others resembled grotesque insects with iridescent wings, and still others possessed bodies that pulsed and shifted in a constant state of flux. Their forms were again fluid, shifting and changing, metamorphosising in front of me. “He is afraid still!” I sensed one say. “He will adjust, don’t worry!” another whispered. And the echo in my mind alerted me to the danger. My eyes, adjusting to the dim light, finally began to focus on more details. And then we were spinning; spinning out of control. Spinning! And the fluttering and squawking began…

With a morbid fascination I realised they were oversized ravens, with feathers the color of midnight and eyes like chips of coal, perched on the high ledges of the cages. Their claws gripped their branches with a frenzied delight. They watched me, their intelligent gaze assessing, judging. A moment of recognition. I had seen smaller versions when I first entered the wood, in search of forest bathing and a restoration of harmony within my troubled world. I was afraid. They clearly sensed my fear, my vulnerability, my utter helplessness. I tried to scream but found my vocal cords useless, choked by the suffocating fear that threatened to drown me! I was drowning in a sea of feathers. The ravens were everywhere; their liquid ink eyes, tiny points of darkness, pinpointing me across the great chasm of this new reality.

A chilling premonition settled upon me, one of terrible metamorphosis, of a change that lay beyond my understanding, a transformation that promised horror beyond imagining. I was theirs now. And I screamed and screamed and screamed only for them to scream back, stabbing my mind with their menace. The chilling serenity wasn't the end. It was a deceptive calm before a deeper, more unsettling storm. The physical transformation, horrific as it was, was only one layer of the alien intrusion. There were subtler, more insidious changes taking place, alterations not of flesh and bone but of mind and will.

Chapter 4: Human Zoo.

"Look after your planet. When you return, this is the message!" Huge ebony, almond eyes telepathically communicated this message to me. It reverberated through every pore, every part of my being. "Look after your planet!" this time I received the instruction with a sense of urgency.

I suddenly realized how the animals at the zoo feel…especially the more intelligent forms of life, as I felt a reserved self-consciousness, aware of being watch by all the strange beings, seemingly entrance with my life form. Humanity displays such arrogance when naively believing in superiority to all other species. I clung to a fragment of hope, as the implication was that I was returning to Earth.

Sickness dwelled within the deep pit of my stomach. I heaved and heaved and heaved. Suddenly I vomited feathers. Strange feathers all around me. A searing pain gripped my hand, and as I glanced down, I noticed a feather sprouting from my ring finger. The cloud of rationality deserted me. I was metamorphosizing, wracked with pain and more and more jet feathers covered me. My lips began to harden, a semi beak began to grow, and clawed feet of sorts stretched in front of me. I was becoming a raven, and The Things were laughing, shaking with hysteria. They were pointing at me.
"Tell the others to look after your planet!" Again, the message was loud and clear but tinged with high amusement. Their laughter now enveloped me, stung me, whipped me with fear! I couldn't speak, only croak! I couldn't move!

Thud!

I was perched in a tree, in the forest from which it began.

My world exploded. One moment, I was surrounded by the pulsating walls and the metallic tang of the alien air, the next, I was sprawled on damp earth, the scent of pine and damp soil assaulting my nostrils. The transition was instantaneous, jarring, like stepping from a nightmare directly into a violently contrasting reality. The familiar sounds of a terrestrial forest – rustling leaves, the distant chirping of crickets – were overwhelming, each noise a sharp, almost painful reminder of my return. Something kept me there; something refused to let me go; something.

Subtle changes occurred, slowly at first, almost imperceptible. I noticed my skin felt different; drier, rougher, like the texture of aged parchment. Sleep offered little respite; my dreams were plagued by visions of the alien human zoo, the pulsating walls, the ravens, the horrifying hopelessness I had witnessed in my fellow captives – if that is what they were. These images were vivid and disturbing, playing out before my eyes like a nightmarish film. The nightmarish visuals intensified as days turned to nights, becoming more intense and vivid, further blurring the line between dream and reality.

One morning, I woke to find a single, dark feather nestled amongst my hair. Panic seized me, cold and paralyzing. My attempts to pluck it out were met with a searing pain, a sharp, almost electric shock that shot through my scalp. There was something inherently alien about this pain. It was not the typical ache or burn of a human injury. It was more akin to the piercing, pulsating metallic tang of the alien air, a pain directly interwoven with the unsettling metallic taste of my experience in the alien zoo.

Over the next few days, more feathers appeared, sprouting from my scalp like dark, menacing thorns. They were initially sparse, interspersed with my human hair, but their numbers increased exponentially. The tingling sensation intensified, spreading to my shoulders, my arms, my legs. It felt as if something was growing beneath my skin, pushing its way outwards, forcing its way into my human form, taking away the reality of my physical being, bit by bit.

The transformation was not limited to my physical form. My senses were becoming altered, heightened. I could hear sounds from an impossible distance, detect scents that were previously imperceptible. My vision seemed sharper, more acute, as if I were viewing the world through a lens that had been recalibrated to perceive a different spectrum of reality.
My body ached, every muscle screaming in protest at the sudden shift. The feathers, now thick and coarse, prickled against my skin, a constant, irritating reminder of the transformation that had taken root within me. I tried to sit up, but my limbs felt heavy, unresponsive, as if weighed down by some unseen force. The grey pallor of my skin was accentuated by the harsh sunlight filtering through the trees. My reflection, when I finally managed to catch a glimpse of it in a puddle of rainwater, was horrifying. The transformation was far more advanced than I had realized. My face was gaunt, my eyes sunken, my beak-like protrusion growing larger, more defined with each passing moment. The feathers were no longer confined to my scalp and shoulders; they covered my arms and legs, obscuring my human form beneath a thick, dark shroud.

The forest, once a symbol of peace and tranquillity, now felt alien, menacing. The towering trees seemed to loom over me, their branches reaching out like skeletal fingers, their shadows twisting and contorting into grotesque shapes. Even the gentle rustling of the leaves sounded sinister, like whispers from some unseen presence. Fear once again smirked at me. I was not just different; I was an alien in my own world.

I stumbled through the undergrowth, my movements clumsy and awkward. The new appendages, the growing feathers, hampered my progress, making even the simplest tasks a monumental effort. The world seemed to shift and distort around me, objects blurring at the edges of my vision. My sense of direction was gone; the familiar landscape had become a labyrinth of shadows and uncertainty. My thoughts were fragmented, my memories fractured, the line between reality and hallucination dissolving.

The metallic tang that had permeated the alien air still lingered, now a phantom taste on my tongue, a constant, nagging reminder of my ordeal. It seemed to be interwoven with my very being, a permanent marker of my captivity. The pulsing light, though absent, still vibrated faintly within my skull, a rhythmic echo of the alien prison.

Days blurred into nights. I found myself drawn to the darkness, seeking refuge in the shadows of the forest. The change was accelerating; my human form was rapidly receding, replaced by something monstrous, something that was no longer human. My hands, once capable of delicate tasks, were now clumsy, covered in coarse feathers, ending in wickedly curved talons. My feet were transformed, becoming more and more like bird-like talons than human feet, the transition adding a strange, terrifyingly agile grace to my movements. Every day there were more subtle changes.

The oversized ravens were now gone, yet their presence continued to haunt me. I could feel their spectral gaze upon me, a chilling reminder of their sinister role in my transformation. Their image and their disturbing silence were forever imprinted on my mind. Their unseen watching became a constant, unnerving presence that never seemed to fully dissipate. I could sense them, even when I couldn't see them, their silent observation a heavy weight on my very existence.

Food was a challenge; my beak was not yet fully formed, making eating near impossible. I tried to tear at berries and insects, but my clumsy attempts were largely unsuccessful. Hunger gnawed at me, a constant, gnawing pain that added to the overall agony of my transformation. The transformation was not just physical, it was a profound alteration of my being – my senses, my instincts, my very essence.

After a while I felt a connection to the other avian creatures in the forest, a kinship that both terrified and strangely comforted me. Their calls resonated within me, a part of their song seeming to echo a lost portion of my own consciousness. I found myself mimicking their calls, the sounds emerging as guttural croaks and harsh caws. It felt... right, somehow, even though it was a horrifyingly alien sound to make.

One evening, while perched atop a high branch, watching the sunset over the forest, I felt a strange shift within me. A sensation of completion, of finality. The metamorphosis was nearing its conclusion. My once human hands had completely vanished, replaced by fully developed wings. The transformation, previously a series of jarring steps, had become a smooth and seamless change. I felt no pain, no distress, merely an unsettling sense of inevitability. I spread my new wings, their darkness echoing the blackness of the night. The transformation was now complete, the final and permanent stamp of this alien prison seared onto my being.

The world was different now. My perspective altered, distorted by my avian form. The forest floor seemed far below. The rustling of leaves no longer felt threatening, but like familiar voices speaking a language I suddenly understood. My senses, once painfully acute, had mellowed, yet they were more attuned to the rhythms of nature, its scents, its sounds.
But the memories remained. The pulsating walls, the metallic tang, the obsidian eyes of the ravens, the other humans – or what remained of them – were forever etched into my consciousness, a haunting reminder of my captivity and a terrifying testament to the alien's brutal experiment.

I was no longer human; I was a living embodiment of the horror I had endured. And as the darkness cloaked me, as the moon replaced the sun in the vast expanse of night sky, I knew that I would never truly escape the alien zoo. It lived within me, in the chilling rhythm of my new existence, a silent, pulsating prison of feathers and bone. The Earth, once my home, was now merely a landscape, as foreign and hostile as the planet from which I had so unexpectedly and terrifyingly returned. The transformation was complete, and my new reality was only just beginning. The horror, once external, now resided within, a permanent part of my very being, a chilling reminder of my permanent, feathery captivity.

The whole transformation began subtly, almost imperceptibly. A faint tingling sensation, like a thousand tiny spiders crawling beneath my skin. At first, I dismissed it as fatigue, the lingering effects of my ordeal. The forest, still a source of both comfort and unease, offered little respite. The shadows seemed deeper, the sounds more acute, as if my senses were being recalibrated to a new frequency. I found myself flinching at the sudden chirp of a cricket, the rustling of leaves becoming a symphony of unsettling whispers.

The sunlight, once a welcome warmth, now felt harsh, almost painful. I sought refuge in the deeper recesses of the woods, the dappled shade offering a temporary reprieve from the incessant assault on my senses. But even in the darkness, the tingling persisted, growing stronger, more insistent. It began to concentrate on my scalp, a prickling sensation that spread across my skin like an insidious vine.

I tried to rationalize it, to explain it away as a side effect of the trauma, a psychosomatic response to the horrors I had witnessed. I told myself it was stress, the result of my isolation, the overwhelming fear that still clung to me like a shroud. I desperately clung to the hope that this was temporary, a fleeting symptom that would eventually disappear. However, deep down, a cold dread began to take root, whispering insidious doubts in the darkest corners of my mind.

The changes were causing other issues as well. Eating became increasingly difficult. My appetite waned, and the food I managed to consume caused sharp pains in my throat, as if my body was rejecting it as a foreign substance. My sleeping patterns were also affected by the ongoing transformations; I found that I could stay awake for longer periods of time, with sleep being less necessary to maintain my existence. The transformation felt as if it were continuing even while I slept, changing my physiology at a frighteningly rapid pace.

The rational part of my mind fought back against the horror of this reality. I told myself it was an illness, a rare disease, a hallucination brought on by trauma. But the physical evidence was undeniable. The feathers, the altered senses, the pain, the increasing difficulty in functioning as a human being. The increasing reality of the transformation was undeniable and was rapidly making my existence harder, as if the very air around me was trying to choke me.

I sought refuge in solitude, retreating deeper into the forest, avoiding contact with the outside world. The fear of discovery, of being seen in my altered state, was overwhelming. The thought of others' reactions, of their fear and revulsion, was a constant, agonizing weight on my mind. The mirror became my enemy, reflecting a horror I had previously only imagined.

Days bled into nights, each sunrise a renewed wave of dread. I watched my reflection with a chilling mixture of fascination and horror as the change accelerated. My fingers became completely distorted, the bones shifting, thickening, ending in sharp talons. My skin grew rougher, colder to the touch, the texture more akin to the dark feathers that were littered my body. My feet were those of a bird, my toes fused together, my nails transformed into claws. The transformation didn't just alter my appearance; it was modified my locomotion and agility, bestowing upon me an eerie grace and flight ability, the very thing that made the transformation terrifying.

My thoughts, once clear and rational, became fragmented, muddled, often giving way to the terrifying visions from my traumatic experience in the alien zoo. The constant, pulsing light of the alien prison seemed to be mirrored in the rhythmic throbbing of my own body, a phantom sensation that mirrored the nightmare itself.

Chapter 5: Metamorphosis.

The initial terror, the visceral agony of the metamorphosis, had been a relentless assault on my senses. But the subsequent quietude, the uncanny peace, felt...wrong! Too perfect, too complete. It was a void, yes, but a void crafted with precision, a carefully constructed absence filled with an unsettling stillness. Memories, once vivid and painful, began to fade, not naturally, as if time had eroded them, but as if someone were systematically erasing them, carefully removing the painful details, the human connections. The faces of my loved ones, once etched into my memory, blurred, became indistinct, their emotions muted, their personalities fading into a generalized warmth, a sentimentality devoid of specificity. It wasn't a natural forgetting; it was a targeted amnesia, a surgically precise removal of the parts of my past that the alien influence wished to eliminate. My thoughts, once a chaotic torrent, now seemed…directed. Not in the sense of deliberate control, not a conscious manipulation, but in a subtler, more insidious way. My instincts, my desires, seemed to shift subtly, almost imperceptibly. I found myself drawn to certain places, compelled by unseen forces toward specific actions, my motivations unclear, my impulses unexplainable.

The oversized ravens, reappeared gradually, and joined me as my newfound brethren; they were a crucial part of this disturbing puzzle. They swooped and croaked gleefully encircling me. Their presence, initially terrifying, soon felt…natural. Their caws, once jarring and unsettling, were now a familiar background hum, a constant, comforting presence. I noticed patterns in their behaviour, in their movements, a synchronicity that went beyond mere flocking instinct. They seemed to guide me, to lead me towards certain areas, to deter me from others.

Their seemingly random flights followed specific routes, intricate patterns that only later revealed themselves as carefully orchestrated movements, a silent, avian choreography that seemed to control my actions. They weren't merely companions; they were conductors, silently directing my actions through subtle nudges, imperceptible cues.

One night, perched high in a gnarled oak, the wind rustling through my feathers, a horrifying realization dawned upon me. The transformation was not simply biological; it was a form of mind control, a sophisticated form of subjugation that bypassed the conscious mind, working on a deeper, more primal level. The aliens hadn't just changed my body; they'd reprogrammed my soul, my very essence. The chilling silence that had previously comforted me now felt like a vast, echoing chamber where the alien mind played its insidious music, a symphony of subtle manipulations. It was a silent command, an internalized obedience, a deep, unwavering loyalty to an unseen master. The birds, my brethren, were not merely allies; they were extensions of this alien control, silent enforcers of a dreadful, unspoken servitude. The alien influence worked not through direct commands or obvious manipulations, but through subtle shifts in my perception, subtle alterations in my instincts. It was a form of psychological conditioning so profound that it was almost impossible to detect, a process so carefully executed that it felt...natural. The control was absolute, yet it felt like freedom. The paradox was terrifying.

My memories, or what remained of them, began to morph, to subtly alter, to blend reality with a fabricated narrative, an alien overlay of manufactured experiences. No mortgage worries; no debts; no employment concerns. The line between genuine recollection and carefully implanted memories blurred, creating a disorienting mix of truth and deception. Even my own thoughts felt strangely alien, tainted with unfamiliar concepts, disturbing notions that felt both foreign and completely inherent. My innermost desires, my deepest instincts, seemed to be dictated by an entity far removed from my former humanity, an entity inhabiting the dark corners of my mind, subtly shaping my reality.

The horror wasn't in the grotesque physical transformation; it was in the complete and utter loss of self, the insidious erosion of my autonomy, the subtle, chilling surrender of my will. It was the unsettling realization that I was not just changed, not just transformed, but utterly controlled, my actions, my thoughts, my very being, moulded into a vessel for the alien will. The ravens, my silent accomplices, served as a constant reminder of this alien control, their presence a chilling testament to my own insidious subjugation. Their watchful eyes, their synchronized movements, their haunting caws – all served as a constant, silent affirmation of my altered state.

The planet, once a source of terror and confinement, now felt…familiar. The landscape resonated with an alien harmony, a sinister alignment with my altered perceptions. It wasn't just a foreign world; it was an extension of the alien influence, a perfectly orchestrated stage for their insidious manipulations.

I was a puppet, my strings pulled by invisible hands, my actions dictated by an unseen power. My avian existence was not a liberation, not a freedom, but a carefully constructed prison, a cage built not of bars and walls but of subtle manipulations and carefully implanted instincts.

The sun rose, painting the sky with hues of alien beauty, the beauty of a meticulously crafted illusion. My reflection in a pool of water, a distorted image of a raven, stared back at me, eyes devoid of humanity, eyes reflecting a void where once a soul had resided. The fight wasn't over; it had simply moved to a deeper level, a subterranean struggle within the confines of my own mind, a silent war fought between the fragments of my former self and the insidious presence of the alien controller. This wasn't just a physical transformation; it was a cosmic rape, a total and utter violation of my being, an insidious, silent conquest that left me hollow, a shell of my former self, controlled and manipulated by a force beyond human comprehension.

The loneliness, once a human emotion, had morphed into something far more profound, a cosmic isolation, a terrifying separation not just from humanity but from myself, from the very essence of what it meant to be me. Sleep offered no respite; instead, my dreams were filled with fragmented images, distorted memories, a horrifying collage of alien landscapes, and unsettling encounters with the beings who had wrought this transformation. The line between waking and sleeping blurred, the alien influence seeping into every aspect of my existence, blurring the boundaries of reality itself.

The once comforting darkness now held a sinister undercurrent, the silence amplified by the constant, pervasive presence of the alien mind. The world, once a source of wonder and mystery, had become a prison, a carefully constructed stage for a play of insidious control. Every instinct, every thought, every action was orchestrated by unseen forces, a chilling testament to the pathos of my situation.

There was no hope, no path to escape this insidious mind control. My fate was sealed, my body and mind irrevocably altered, my very essence tainted by the alien touch. The only path forward was to endure, to exist as a vessel, a conduit for the alien will, a prisoner in my own body, a slave in my own mind. The silence of my avian existence had become a chilling symphony of surrender. The transformation was not merely complete; it was absolute. I was their creature, their creation, their perfect, silent slave. And in the depths of that terrible truth, a chilling, alien peace settled in my mind.

The physical transformation, the horrifying metamorphosis into a raven, was merely the outward manifestation of a deeper, more sinister process – a complete and utter takeover of my being. But *why*? The question gnawed at the edges of my altered consciousness, a persistent itch beneath the alien veneer. Was this a mere experiment, a grotesque scientific study on interspecies transformation? Or was it something far greater, a calculated act of cultural assimilation, a colonization not of land but of mind and body?

The ravens, my silent brethren, offered no answers, only a chilling, unwavering presence. Their movements, once seemingly random, now revealed themselves as deliberate, intricate patterns, a complex avian ballet orchestrated by an unseen hand. They were not just companions; they were instruments, extensions of the alien influence, silent witnesses to my gradual erasure. They watched me, their eyes of tar reflecting the alien landscape, mirroring the unsettling transformation unfolding within me.

The forest itself seemed to shift and change, subtly adapting to my altered perceptions. The colors intensified, the sounds sharpened, the very air itself vibrated with an alien energy that resonated within my new bird body. It wasn't merely a foreign world; it was a meticulously crafted environment designed to reinforce the alien influence, to further solidify my subjugation. The very stones seemed to hum with an alien power, a subtle energy that permeated everything, shaping my thoughts, guiding my actions. The stones dripped blood.

Sometimes, in the dead of night, when the wind howled through my feathers like a mournful dirge, flashes of memory would pierce through the alien fog, fragments of my former life, glimpses of humanity, of love, of connection. These were brief, fleeting moments, quickly obscured by the insidious tide of alien influence. They were like ghosts, haunting the periphery of my consciousness, reminding me of what I had lost, of who I had been. These glimpses served not as comfort, but as a constant, agonizing reminder of the profound loss, a reminder of the agonizing transformation. The nights were the worst. The darkness, once a comforting blanket, now pulsed with an alien energy, a sinister hum that seemed to resonate within my very bones. The silence was deafening, broken only by the rhythmic calls of the ravens, their song a constant, chilling reminder of my new reality. In my dreams, if they could be called dreams, I would see elements of the alien ship, the cold, metallic corridors, the disconcerting, oversized ravenlike beings, their eyes filled with an unsettling intelligence, watching, observing, judging. Their deafening silence was more terrifying than any scream.

The real aliens themselves remained elusive, their presence felt more than seen. I never caught a glimpse of them, but their influence was undeniable, pervasive, a constant, subtle pressure shaping my every thought, every action. Their methods were so mysterious and unobtrusive that resistance felt futile, an impossible task. The very fabric of my being was intertwined with their influence, a terrifying symbiosis that defied understanding. The transformation wasn't merely physical; it was spiritual, psychological, a complete and utter erasure of my identity. I was a shell, a vessel for their purposes, my humanity fading, replaced by a chilling, alien emptiness. Even my instincts, once governed by human desires and needs, were now guided by the alien will, my actions predetermined by an unseen force. The raven's innate survival instincts were sharpened, honed, a terrifying efficiency that was both frightening and completely foreign. I could feel the alien intelligence working in tandem with my own basic survival, a partnership of sorts.

Chapter 6: The Aftermath.

Days blurred into nights; each moment indistinguishable from the last. The repetitive nature of my new life was a chilling testament to my imprisonment, the cyclical rhythm of foraging, resting, and watching, all orchestrated by an unseen hand. Even my hunger, my thirst, were dictated by the alien influence, a constant reminder of my utter dependence.

The possibility that this transformation served a larger, more sinister purpose began to consume my thoughts. Perhaps this wasn't merely a scientific experiment, but a deliberate act of colonization, a strategic plan to transform humanity into a new form of life, a biological Trojan horse to infiltrate the planet and its inhabitants. The ravens, acting as both a biological and psychological bridge, were a chilling testament to this idea.

The thought chilled me to the core, even as the chilling alien influence began to dampen my human capacity for fear, replacing it with a strange, almost unnatural tranquillity. It was a disturbing calm, a chilling absence of emotion that felt both foreign and somehow inevitable

With morbid fascination and the chilling realisation grasping me, I resolved that the other 'subjects' in this grotesque avian zoo – humans, like me, had undergone the same horrifying transformation, each stage of metamorphosis just as my own. Their eyes, once filled with terror, had adopted the same unsettling blankness, the same void I saw in my own reflection. We were all prisoners, silent witnesses to a cosmic horror, our humanity slowly being erased, replaced by a chilling, alien emptiness.

There was no resistance, only a chilling, passive acceptance, a terrible resignation to the inevitable. The aliens, whoever or whatever they were, had achieved a complete and utter victory. They had not conquered a world with brute force but through a far more insidious means – the complete and utter alteration of its inhabitants, their minds and bodies transformed into vessels for their own unknown purposes.

And as the sun dipped below this alternative horizon, casting long shadows across the bizarre landscape, I felt a strange sense of peace, a terrible, alien serenity. It was the peace of utter defeat, the quiet acceptance of my own erasure. The transformation was not only complete; it was perfect, a horrifying masterpiece of alien engineering. My human self, once vibrant and full of life, now existed only as a fading memory, a ghostly echo in the silent chamber of my avian mind. The horror wasn't in the transformation itself; it was in the complete and utter loss of self, in the terrifying knowledge that my fate was sealed, my destiny predetermined by a power beyond human comprehension. The alien influence had achieved its purpose. I was no longer me. I was theirs. And the silence, once a source of dread, now felt strangely…right.

The omnipresent eyes of the ravens, large and unnervingly intelligent, followed my every movement. They were always there, perched on grotesque, alien flora or circling overhead in silent, watchful patterns. Their cawing, once a jarring intrusion, now felt like a morbid soundtrack to my transformation, a chilling counterpoint to the unsettling quiet of this alien world. The rhythmic repetition of their calls, a dark, almost hypnotic rhythm, seemed to accelerate the process, pushing me further along the irreversible path to becoming one of them.

It wasn't just their physical presence; it was their sheer *knowingness* that unsettled me, a silent understanding of the process I was undergoing, of the alien influence that was reshaping me. They were not merely observers; they were participants, integral to the unfolding horror. Their intelligence, far beyond anything I'd encountered in terrestrial avian life, suggested a higher level of interaction, a symbiotic relationship with the alien force that had captured me.

The world has shifted, taken on a new perspective, a new dimension. The familiar trees loom taller, their leaves rustle with secrets only I can hear. The air, once stale and ordinary, carries a thousand scents, a thousand subtle messages. My human identity, my human form, is gone, replaced by something beautiful, terrifying, and undeniably alien.

I take flight, a black raven soaring through the twilight sky, a silent observer, a detached witness to the human dramas unfolding below. I am no longer a part of your world, your petty anxieties, your limited perspective. I am an outsider, an alien, a creature of twilight, forever changed by my journey; and with mild amusement I recognize I am liberated. I am home, but home was not where I had been. Home is indeed the sky, the wind, the boundless expanse of the night. Home is in the freedom of flight, in the silent observation of the world from a perspective far beyond human understanding. And in the depths of my being, the new language, a code interwoven into my very DNA, whispered secrets only a raven can comprehend. The transformation is complete. The inevitable return has finally revealed my true nature.

And now I sit and watch the watched who believe they are the superior species – humanity displaying the human condition at its worst. Around me, my liquid, shadowy friends laugh, and smirk, and shake with hysteria…they are laughing and laughing and laughing. They are quietly resolving the problem of humanity's destruction of the earth and their obsession with material things. Over consumerism, exchanging currencies, warring with each other…and the more they laugh, the more humanity shrinks, and will shrink and shrink…to a world of ravens. Our alien friends are among us.

However, fear not…unless of course, you're afraid of flying!

Epilogue.

To the relentless whisper of the uncanny, to the chilling embrace of the unknown, and to the unsettling beauty of metamorphosis. This book is dedicated to those who dare to peer into the abyss and find within it, not only horror, but a strange, unsettling fascination. To those who find themselves drawn to the grotesque, the macabre, and the unsettlingly beautiful, this is for you.

For those who have stared into the face of trauma and found within the wreckage, a spark of resilience, a tenacity to survive, even amidst the decay and disintegration of the self. For those whose minds wander to the fringes of reality, for those who seek stories that explore the darkest corners of the human psyche, and delve into the unsettling transformation of body and soul, this story is offered as a testament to the endurance of the spirit even as it is ravaged by the horrors that dwell beyond the familiar.

This is a dedication to the strange, unsettling, and beautiful metamorphosis of the soul – the journey from human to something...other. It is a tribute to the enduring power of the grotesque, the dark beauty that festers in the shadows and finds its way into the light, twisting and transforming all that it touches. It's an exploration of the boundaries between human and animal, sanity and madness, a recognition of the terrifying and exquisite nature of transformation.

This work is dedicated to the metamorphosis itself, the horrifying and beautiful journey from the known to the unknown, a descent into the darkest depths of the human experience, and the strange, unsettling solace found within the final transformation. This dark fairy tale, a descent into madness and feathers, is for the brave souls who dare to embrace the darkness. It's a tribute to the whispers in the wind, the shadows that dance in the corners of your vision, and the unsettling beauty that hides in the heart of the horrific.

This is to all those who appreciate the haunting blend of science and horror, of the human condition and the chilling unknown. To the readers who seek to explore the very boundaries of the body and the self, this story is a testament to your own courage and curiosity.

Leo John.

Made in United States
North Haven, CT
15 April 2025